BATTLE BUGS

THE BUTTERFLY REBELLION

by **JACK PATTON**

illustrated by **BRETT BEAN**

SCHOLASTIC INC.

With special thanks to Adrian Bott

ISBN 978-0-545-94515-8

10 9 8 7 6 5 4 3 2 1   16 17 18 19 20

Printed in the U.S.A.   40
First printing 2016
Book design by Phil Falco and Ellen Duda

CONTENTS

EARTHWORM WARNING

"Okay, you greedy birds," Max Darwin said as he pulled the roll of netting over to the blueberry plot. "Let's see you get through this!"

The three birds sitting on top of Grandpa Mike's shed stared down at him. There was a look in their beady black eyes that he didn't like one bit.

"They're just normal birds," he told himself, shuddering. "Hungry birds that want to eat Grandpa's juicy berries, that's all."

Max knew there was no need to be anxious around creatures that were so much smaller than him. Yet, ever since a flock of vermilion flycatchers had nearly eaten him alive on Bug Island, he'd always felt uneasy around birds.

He unrolled a long piece of the plastic netting and pulled it all the way over the tops of the blueberry bushes. Next, he worked his way around the edges, pegging the net into place.

Grandpa Mike's garden had been a magical place for Max for as long as he could remember. His earliest memory was of reaching out for a strawberry, gleaming like a jewel in the sunshine, and seeing a magnificent green insect standing on top of it like a guardian. Ever since, he'd been fascinated by bugs and all things creepy-crawly.

"That should do it," he said, glancing up at the shed. No greedy bird was going to get its beak on his grandpa's precious blueberries now.

Just then, a delicious smell wafted over from the nearby house. Max's mouth watered at the thought of the meal to come. Collard greens, cornbread, macaroni and cheese, bacon . . . all cooked up like only Grandpa Mike could.

As if on cue, his grandpa's face appeared at the window. "Food's on the table for any hardworking young man that wants to come and get it!" he called.

Max moved fast. He pushed in the last of the pegs, stomped them down with his foot, and sprinted back toward the house. Inside, the spread on the table made him grin. He settled in by the window so he could look out at the garden, grabbed his fork, and waited for Grandpa Mike to join him.

"Dig in, Maxwell. You've earned it," his grandfather said, sitting down.

Max grinned, loaded up a huge forkful of mac and cheese, and devoured it. Soon, he was completely stuffed.

After lunch, as they were clearing the table, Max peered out at the garden and up to the shed. *Sorry, my feathered friends,* he thought. *You're going hungry today.*

What he saw made his eyes go wide. The birds weren't going hungry at all. Instead, they were swooping down and attacking the netting, ripping at it with their beaks and plucking the berries through the holes. *And* they looked pretty smug about it, too.

Anger overtook him and he ran outside, waving his arms wildly.

"Max, come back. We'll double up the netting after my nap!"

Max ignored his grandfather's words. He shouted at the birds and they flew up, squawking rudely at him. They frantically flapped their way back onto the shed, giving him a look that said, "We'll be back for more just as soon as you turn your back."

Max drooped down and stared at his feet, breathing hard. All his work was for nothing. Even the worms seemed to be laughing at him. They were sitting up and jiggling around.

Wait, what?

He took a closer look. Earthworms were poking up from the ground, waving their pink bodies as if they were trying to get Max's attention.

"Bug Island," Max whispered. "They must need me over there, now!"

Panic gripped him as he tried to remember where he'd left his magic book. *The Complete Encyclopedia of Arthropods* wasn't

just a bug reference guide; it was the gateway to a magical world. Once inside, Max would shrink down to bug size and join his friends, a group of intelligent talking bugs. As human adviser to the bug forces, he'd helped out many times in their war against the reptiles of Reptile Island.

He wracked his brain. *When did I use it last?*

Suddenly, he had it. It was when he was looking up a spider of some sort . . . a spider among the timbers of Grandpa Mike's shed!

He stared hard at the birds perched on the roof as he threw the shed door open. "Don't worry," he said. "I'll be coming back for you!"

He pulled the door closed behind him and dashed to the encyclopedia that lay on the workbench. It was already open to the map of Bug Island, as if it had been waiting for him, and the pages were lighting up the dark shed with their misty golden glow.

Max took the all-important magnifying glass out of his pocket and drew closer. He held the magnifying glass over the map and in an instant was snatched off his feet. The call was a powerful one this time.

Must be important, he thought.

He whirled around, becoming smaller and smaller, as he was pulled into Bug Island once again . . .

FORBIDDEN GLADE

Usually when Max landed on Bug Island, he didn't have a clue where he was. This time was different.

As he tumbled through the warm air, he was met with thick, twisted branches and dangling vines. The ground below was richly carpeted with bobbing ferns, long snaking roots, and plants in striking colors.

th…

away.

Max smacked

he fell, and suddenly cam

halt, landing on a soft surface.

the rain forest—

couldn't be

twigs as

brupt

"Phew!" he said as he sat up. "That was some ride."

He looked around him and saw he was on a spongy, bright scarlet flower. Long green spikes rose up in front of him like a row of needle-sharp teeth. Max pulled his hands off the sticky surface and waited for the plant to stop bobbing up and down.

Something about the plant seemed familiar, but Max couldn't quite tell what it was. The sweet, sugary scent rising from

g friends

it was amazi ar delicious.

would prob he wondered. The

Wher smelled almost as good as

exoti Mike's cooking. *This should be*

Gr

paradise!

Max suddenly felt uneasy as he looked down at the plant's bright red interior and across at the long needle-like spines. Above him was a second set of long green prongs, hovering right over his head.

"Uh-oh," Max murmured as he realized what he was sitting on. He'd landed right in the gaping jaws of a gigantic Venus flytrap.

He knew that Venus flytraps had special trigger hairs inside them—the ones hovering over him at that very instant. Touching

one hair wouldn't do anything, but to
ing two in a row would snap the jaws s
Then, whatever the plant had trapped inside
would be digested alive. No wonder the
bugs didn't like it here—they could easily
become dinner for a huge carnivorous plant!

"Don't move," he told himself through
gritted teeth. The jaws of the plant were
still wide open—if he just kept still and put
his brain to use, he might have a chance.

Max slowly raised his left foot. One of
the trigger hairs was crushed beneath it.

"I must have landed on it when I fell,"
he said miserably. "That's my one strike
used up . . ."

He could clearly see the other trigger
hairs sprouting like dark whiskers from the

plant's juicy red inside. They should be enough to avoid, if he could just go slo and resist the urge to run for his life.

Max carefully moved across to the side of the jaws, steering clear of the trigger hairs. His sneakers made squishing sounds, and sweet juices bubbled up underfoot.

He came to the edge and readied himself to jump. A breeze wobbled the whole plant. As he struggled to regain his balance, he grabbed out for the first thing he could find.

Suddenly, he let go in horror: It was a trigger hair! But before Max could blink, the great green jaws closed with astonishing speed. He flung himself into the air, but the jaws closed on his foot, leaving him dangling from the mouth of the hungry flytrap.

"Argh!" he cried. "Get off me!" He wiggled and struggled until his foot came free with a noisy slurp and he landed, gasping, in the leafy mulch below.

Picking himself up, he saw the whole area was overgrown with sinister-looking plants. Venus flytraps' spiny jaws gaped like alien life-forms. Pitcher plants glistened invitingly, offering any passing bug all the nectar they could drink—at the price of being plunged into a stomach full of digestive fluid. Sundews lay in wait, the tips of their tentacles glistening with gluey drops. Max knew what would happen if he brushed against one. The plant's tentacles would close like a

fist, trapping him inside a sticky mass wi
no hope of escape.

This isn't bug paradise, Max thought.
It's a bug graveyard!

Max ran as quickly as he could through
flowers that towered high above him. Up
ahead were the flat leaves of a Mimosa
plant, looking like the feathers on an arrow
shaft. Max ran down the plant's entire length
like a high wire at the circus. Its leaves
furled up behind him as he passed, clutching like fingers.

His chest ached from running. He caught
sight of a clearing up ahead and sprinted
toward it. It seemed free from carnivorous
plants. Hopefully there wasn't something
even worse lurking in wait . . .

Max staggered into the clearing and ran right into something colorful towering above him. It had four enormous bluish-green petals: two large ones above and two smaller ones below.

As Max looked up, the "petals" twitched. *They aren't petals, they're wings!* he thought, amazed.

The plant wasn't a plant at all. It was a butterfly—but it dwarfed any other butterfly Max had ever met before!

"You've finally come," the butterfly said. "I knew you would one day. I knew I could not hide from the war forever."

"Excuse me?" Max asked, confused. He was panting and out of breath.

"You are Max? General Barton's adviser?"

"That's me."

"My name is Alexis."

That name rang very loud bells in Max's memory. "You're a Queen Alexandra's birdwing, aren't you? The biggest butterfly in the world!"

"I am." Alexis sighed. "I was a warrior once, but no longer."

"Why?" Max asked cautiously, wondering how a bug with no visible weapons could be a warrior.

Alexis was silent for a moment, then he sighed again. "We birdwings were elite battle transports when the lizards first began attacking. We would fly into battle with other bugs on our backs, bringing them within striking distance. We carried scorpions, spiders, even centipedes."

"You must have been awesome!" Max said.

"We were," Alexis said. "We were so effective that the reptiles were determined to wipe us out. They ambushed us with a deadly attack. I was the only survivor."

Max understood. "So you hid away from the war."

"Yes. General Barton assigned me to watch over the Forbidden Glade, where it's quiet."

"I see," Max said, feeling deeply sorry for the beautiful creature. "I know that you want to stay away from the fight, but I could use your help to get out of here. There are carnivorous plants everywhere."

"I haven't transported anyone in a long time," Alexis said doubtfully.

Max peered into the glade. The walk to the bug camp would take longer than getting a ride, but it wasn't impossible. "I guess I'll walk then, and take my chances with the Venus flytraps."

As Max turned to go, Alexis let out a cry of alarm.

"Look!" he said.

Max tilted his head up. In the distance he could just make out a shadow crossing the sky. Dark shapes were flying from the direction of Reptile Island, headed straight for the center of the forest. And they were *fast*.

"Birds!" he gasped. "I have to warn Barton."

Max quickened his pace through the deep foliage, but was soon stopped by a deep voice behind him.

"Wait!" Alexis called. "I want to help you."

"What do you mean?" Max asked.

"I may no longer be in the trenches," Alexis started, "but I'm still a Battle Bug. Climb aboard."

Max smiled in relief and clambered onto Alexis's body. In an instant, the huge, color-ful wings began to whir, and Max launched into the sky.

BATTLE STATIONS!

Moments later, Max and Alexis touched down in the center of General Barton's camp, among a crowd of excited bugs. The insects should have been at battle stations like usual, but instead they were wandering around like they were on vacation.

"Max!" called Spike, the emperor scorpion and Max's best friend. "Arriving in style, eh? And on a birdwing, too. I haven't seen one of those in years! You're just in time . . ."

Max was about to ask, "In time for what?" but he never got the chance.

A dark shadow swept across the sky. Then came another and another. Fearful bugs looked up, and cries of alarm rang out.

Max looked at Spike. "I was about to tell you, but . . ." Max started.

"Take cover!" Spike roared above Max. "The birds are back!"

All at once, the birds came swooping in, screeching as they flew. They let out a war cry that sent the smaller bugs running in fright. As they came closer, Max got his first clear look at them. They were slender, with long tail feathers and brightly colored plumage.

Max gasped. "Bee-eaters!" Like the name suggested, these dangerous birds were a bug's worst nightmare. Their preferred snack of choice: flying insects.

"Battle stations!" Spike shouted. "Bombardier beetles to the towers. Mantises, stand by to grab any birds that come close enough."

Max bravely stood his ground and looked up at the oncoming bird forces. They were coming in low, almost brushing the treetops.

In seconds, the Battle Bugs were ready. Stern-faced bugs stood on all the walkways and guard towers. They knew what to expect. The birds would make a power dive and snatch up as many bugs as they could. That would be the land bugs' only chance to attack them.

"We need flyers! Where's Buzz and her squadron?"

"Practicing formation flight," Spike grunted.

"What? Why on earth would Buzz waste time with that fancy stuff when the lizards could strike at any moment?" Max asked.

"She didn't know there was going to be a bird attack, little buddy. The lizards have been very quiet lately!" Spike said.

Any second now, the birds would be upon them. Max grabbed a heavy piece of wood and climbed onto Spike's back, ready for the fight.

The birds kept coming until they drastically changed course and went swooping over the Battle Bugs' heads and on across the forest—missing the camp completely.

"They're not attacking," Spike said as he watched the birds swoop past the camp. "I'm very confused."

"Me, too."

"I don't like it when I'm confused."

Max squinted after the birds. Was this just a scouting mission?

Then he realized he'd missed something.

"Spike, I think they're carrying *passengers!*"

Max shielded his eyes from the sun. Every one of the birds had a little lizard clinging to it. As Max watched, the lizards sprang off the birds and spread their arms and legs out. Broad flaps of skin fanned out between their limbs and their bodies, letting them glide on the air. Like paratroopers, they sailed gently down to the top of the forest canopy. Once they were safely among the uppermost branches, they clung to the bark and wiggled out of sight.

"There's only one kind of lizard that can glide like that," Max said. "Draco flying lizards." *Draco* meant "dragon," he remembered. Even though they didn't breathe fire, they were still fearsome reptiles.

With their flying lizard passengers dropped off, the birds wheeled around and went winging back the way they'd come. *Back to Reptile Island*, thought Max, *to report to whatever new commander is running things over there.* General Komodo had fallen, but others had tried to take his place, such as the crocodile Longtooth.

"Where did they go?" a mantis sentry asked.

"It looks like they're hiding in the trees," Max said.

"Permission to lead a force up there to check things out, sir?"

"Permission denied," Max said firmly. "For all we know, that's exactly what they want us to do. By the time we get our bugs up there, they could have flown to a new location—or worse, picked half of us off!"

The mantis was about to protest, but Spike shook a threatening pincer at him. "You heard Max. With General Barton away, he's the senior commander here. So you do as he says."

Max blinked. "Barton's away? Where is he?"

Spike mumbled something and shuffled his feet.

"Spike?"

"He's having his shell polished," Spike said.

Max stood dumbfounded. "Are you serious? Buzz is doing loop-the-loops, Barton's polishing his shell . . . I suppose Webster's weaving a party banner?"

"Close," Spike grunted. "It's a military banner."

"A military banner?" Max asked.

"For the parade! I've been trying to tell you since you got here!" Spike burst out. "There's no emergency . . . Well, there is *now*, but there wasn't before. We're having a grand military parade tomorrow to keep everybody's spirits up and show our enemies we're not to be messed with. Obviously, you are invited. It wouldn't be the same without you."

Max smiled and patted the big scorpion on the head. "Thanks, buddy. Sounds like you went to a lot of trouble."

"Barton's at the parade ground on the other side of the forest," Spike said, sounding happier now.

Alexis glanced up at the trees and frowned. "The parade's tomorrow, you say? Fine time for a group of flying lizards to show up."

Spike gasped. "We can't let them spoil General Barton's big day! That would really hurt morale."

Max nodded slowly and patted Spike's head again. "You're right, Spike. We've got to do something about this new threat, and fast."

"Why not just cancel the parade?" asked a ladybug.

Murmurs and buzzes went through the Battle Bugs' ranks.

"She's got a point," whispered a katydid.

"We'd be asking for trouble if we went ahead," hummed a tiny gnat scout.

"Just making ourselves a target," bubbled a water boatman.

"No way!" Max said firmly. Silence fell, and all the bugs looked at him. "The whole point of the parade is to show the reptiles we're not afraid of them. If we canceled it, we wouldn't be bugs at all, we'd be chickens. So we should have it just like you planned!"

A cheer went up among the crowd.

"Well done," Alexis whispered.

"Thanks."

"You made the right decision. The brave decision. But there are still lizards in those trees. What do you plan to do about it?" the butterfly asked.

"We need to scout out that part of the forest. Send word to Buzz. I want the Insect Air Force up in those trees as soon as possible. Spike, you lead the ground force. If any of the Draco lizards have glided down to the ground, I want to know about it."

"Roger that, sir!" Spike answered.

"What about me?" Alexis asked.

Max stared. "You want to volunteer?"

"Good bugs are putting themselves in danger," Alexis said quietly. "I want to return to my glade, but I cannot stand by and do nothing while others risk their lives."

Max beamed. "Can you fly me up to the treetops where the Dracos landed?"

Alexis hesitated. "Just us? You don't want to wait for Buzz and the IAF?"

"There's no time," Max said. "We need information now!"

Alexis bent down so Max could climb aboard. "Hop on. It has been too long since my flying skills were put to the test."

They took off from the bug camp battlements and flew up and up. Alexis went around in a spiral, gaining height all the time, as if they were climbing a gigantic staircase. Soon they were high above the clearing.

Max glanced over his shoulder, hoping Buzz and the rest of the IAF would be there soon. There was no sign of them. The leafy canopy could be hiding anything.

"Okay, Alexis. Let's head in."

The huge butterfly plunged into the leafy branches.

To Max's horror, they instantly had to swerve out of the way of a mass of webbing that crisscrossed their path.

"What's that doing there?"

"Must be some kind of air defense against the birds!" Alexis replied.

Max wanted to turn around, but they were already too far in among the trees. All around them, sticky webbing cables threaded from branch to branch. Living vines had been worked into the barriers. The spiders had obviously been building up the defenses around the camp—it was super difficult to get through.

Alexis dived suddenly, desperately dodging a thick web-line. Max had to grab hold of his antennae to keep from falling off his back. Alexis swerved again, almost too late. Blue-green dust from his wings was left behind on the tree he'd come too close to.

After too many close calls, they finally flew out from among the last of the web-laden branches. Max breathed a sigh of relief.

"The birds would have had trouble flying through that mess," Alexis said. "That must be why they flew *above* the forest, and dropped the Dracos down. Sneaky!"

They flew between the silent, tangled tree branches. Shafts of light lit up the leaves, showing no lizards waiting to attack. The branches, too, were empty.

"Get a little closer and check the trunks," Max suggested.

Alexis fluttered as close as he dared to the tree trunks, one after the other. There was no sign of any of the Draco lizards.

"I guess they moved to a new hideout pretty quickly after they landed. Let's head down to the ground and meet up with Spike."

"Good plan. I can't wait to be out of this place."

Alexis began his descent. Max took a last look up into the trees—and felt his whole body go cold.

A Draco lizard was headed right for them! Wings spread, claws out, it hissed as it flew. Max yelled in alarm as a claw caught his shirt and wrenched him sideways.

He went toppling backward off Alexis's back, and down toward the forest floor that seemed an impossible distance below . . .

TREETOP TERROR

Max tumbled through the air, his limbs thwacking off tree branches as he went. The Draco lizard grabbed hold of a branch and watched with glee as Max plummeted to the ground. Alexis's blue, sail-like wings were a blur as the butterfly sped down toward him.

"Max, spread out!" Alexis shrieked.

Max instantly understood. Like the Draco lizards had done, he spread his arms and legs as wide as he could. He felt the air whoosh into his shirt, making it billow out. The wind resistance wouldn't stop his fall, but hopefully it would slow him down just enough for Alexis to get to him.

Alexis swooped alongside Max, his wings beating so fast the dust went flying off them. "Got to time this right," he cried. He lunged underneath Max.

Whump.

Max landed right in the middle of Alexis's back.

"Thanks for the save," Max panted. "Let's get out of here!"

"I would, but I don't think *he* is going to let us."

Max looked up. The Draco lizard was snarling at them. The next second, it came gliding down, ready to tear them both out of the sky.

"This time, I'll gulp you down in one bite!" he hissed.

Max thought quickly. "Alexis, bring me near that branch."

As the butterfly passed by, Max caught hold of a protruding twig and broke it off. Now at least he had a weapon.

The Draco came charging at them, seeming more dragon-like than ever . . . but Max had a lance now, just like a real knight. He

leveled it at the oncoming lizard. The lizard's sharp claws came clutching for him, but Max thrust his twig into the lizard's face and shoved him away.

The lizard screeched in anger. He fell past them, twisting in the air like a fighter jet shot out of the sky, and vanished into the leaves.

"Alexis, I know how we can win this!" Max said. "He's a glider, but you're a flyer."

"How does that help us?"

"He has to leap from tree to tree, so he loses height each time. He can't go higher unless he climbs back up the tree. But we can fly wherever we want. We just have to keep this fight going until we force him down to the ground!"

The Draco lizard was on the attack again. He leaned down for greater speed, plunging at them like a harrier hawk. His jaws gaped, ready to snatch Max off Alexis's back.

Max got his twig ready again, but the Draco veered from side to side, just as if they were two planes in a dogfight. Max couldn't take aim or be sure of a solid hit. Inspiration struck him, and at the last minute, he changed his grip so that he was holding the twig like a sword.

The Draco came at him. With a yell, Max swung the twig up under his head and landed a solid blow.

This time, the Draco flipped in the air and lost control. He tried to catch a branch, missed, and instead slammed into the tree trunk.

"Yes!" Max yelled. "Got him!"

The lizard frantically tried to change course, but he was plunging down too fast and the only tree he could have clung to was well out of reach. He crashed into the ground and plowed a little furrow in the dead leaves.

Max and Alexis landed beside him. The stunned lizard looked up at them. His eyeballs were wobbling around in his head. Then they focused on Max.

"I know about you Draco lizards," Max said. "You're comfortable up in trees or in the air, but on the ground it's a different story. Isn't that right?"

The lizard slowly backed away from them. "I can still take the pair of you on," he boasted.

"Try it," Alexis growled.

They advanced on the nervous lizard until they had backed him up against a large tree. He glanced around, as if he were hoping for backup from his lizard friends. None came.

"This fight's over and you lost," Max said. "Now tell us what you're doing here."

"Wh-why should I?" stammered the lizard.

"Because if you don't tell us," Max began, "we'll march you back to our camp and keep you prisoner. There's a black widow spider named Jet who's in charge of the bug jail. She could eat you for breakfast!"

"Literally," Alexis added.

The lizard cowered. "No! Not a black widow! I'll tell you anything you want to know!"

Suddenly, a piercing noise rang out across the forest. It was a cicada blast from one of the signaling groups that General Barton had set up. Three more short blasts came, then a pause, then three more.

"That's a warning signal," Alexis said, fluttering up into the air. "Bugs in danger!"

Max turned to face the direction the signal was coming from. "It's the watchtower on the Howling Cliffs. They must be under attack."

While their backs were turned, the lizard quickly skittered up the side of the tree. He let out a mocking laugh. Max turned around and ran at it, yelling, but it was too late. The lizard was already climbing high above his head, vanishing into the leafy branches.

"As if I'd ever tell you bugs anything!" he sneered. "The reptile plans are underway. You couldn't stop us now if you tried."

The cicada alarm signal kept blasting out across the forest. Max and Alexis looked at each other in confusion.

"Should we go after him?" Alexis asked.

Max shook his head. "There's not enough time. Let's get to the watchtower. Sounds like they're in big trouble."

Alexis took off and flew as fast as he

could, weaving between the tree trunks and branches.

"Good thing the signal's so loud. It must carry for a long distance," Alexis said.

They flew out of the forest above the Howling Cliffs, where the watchtower stood looking out toward Reptile Island. It was made of termite mound material, and it had withstood several reptile attacks. Until now . . .

"Oh, no!" Max called out as he and Alexis approached. He stared in horror as he saw the huge chunk missing from the tower's side. The most important defensive structure on all of Bug Island looked like it was about to go crashing into the sea and take a whole bunch of Battle Bugs with it!

TOWER DEFENSE

As they got closer, Max could see the culprits: Draco lizards, swarming all over the watchtower.

"So that's what they're doing here," Max cried. "They're trying to take down our defenses."

Max and Alexis flew toward the tower. From the forest, a fresh wave of Dracos launched themselves into the air. They silently glided down to the watchtower and instantly began to tear the walls away.

"Listen!" yelled Alexis. "That sound. Do you hear it?"

At first, Max heard nothing but the deafening blasts of the cicadas, still sounding the alarm. Then he noticed a steady hum, growing louder and louder. It was the sound of thousands of whirring bug wings.

"It's the Insect Air Force!" he yelled.

"They must have heard the alarm and come to help. Let's hope they're not too late."

Max looked over his shoulder to see an astounding sight. The entire IAF had taken wing and was rushing to the watchtower's aid. They formed an immense cloud of flying insects: bees, wasps, and hornets, along with flying ants, dragonflies, crane flies, and common houseflies. Even the deadly tarantula hawks were there.

Just then, a familiar black-and-gold figure zoomed into view. "Good to see you, Max!" called Buzz the hornet. "What's the situation?"

"It's bad. The lizards are tearing the tower to pieces, and more of them keep flying down out of the forest. We have to stop them somehow."

"Can we cut off their reinforcements?" Alexis suggested.

"Good plan. Buzz, tell the non-stinging bugs to fly back and forth by the edge of the forest. I want a constant stream. With any luck, the lizards won't be able to fly through." *Like traffic on a busy road*, he thought.

"Roger that," chirped Buzz. "And the tower?"

"Bring the hornets to the front for a mass power dive. Our only chance is to sting as many of them as we can and hope the others get scared off."

"On it!"

Max got his twig-lance ready. The hornets lined up in an arrowhead formation, while the flies zoomed over to barricade the forest.

"On my mark," Buzz ordered. "Three, two, one . . . *dive!*"

Alexis followed the screaming hornets down toward the tower. Max's face stung from the wind. The termites inside the tower looked up, saw the hornets coming, and threw themselves into the fight with fresh courage.

The Draco lizards that were munching away at the tower didn't see the hornets until it was too late. Suddenly, they were engulfed in a buzzing, stinging storm of insects. Max saw Buzz deliver three quick, hard stings to the biggest of the Dracos. The lizard hissed in pain, curled up, and fell off the side of the tower.

Max watched him bounce off the edge of the cliff and go tumbling down toward the sea. The lizard only just spread his wing-flaps in time. He glided a short way, then clung to a rock, shivering.

"Second wave, *dive!*" Buzz called.

More hornets came swooping in. The panicked Draco lizards ran around in confusion, which made them an even easier target. Alexis hovered close to the tower wall so that Max could knock the lizards off with his twig. At the foot of the tower, more and more wiggling lizards were retreating.

The tower made an ominous groaning noise. Max looked up and saw the tower top lean over a few inches. Hastily, the termites ran and plastered fresh globs of gluey mud into place, helping to shore up the building.

Over by the forest, Max's plan was working. The thick cloud of swarming flies was impossible for the Dracos to steer through. One or two tried to glide down to join the attack on the tower, but the flies buffeted and jostled them until they flopped down for a crash landing.

That's the trouble with gliding, Max thought. *You can only ever go down, not up.*

"Keep attacking," Buzz shouted as she speared yet another lizard with her stinger. The Dracos were scuttling around to the other side of the tower, closer to the cliff top and the sea.

"I agree," Max said. "Send in a fresh wave of stingers—better make it the wasps, since they can sting multiple times."

"Good plan."

"And see if Dobs and the other giant dobsonflies can pull some of those Dracos off the tower with their big mandibles."

"I love the way you think!" Buzz waved her antennae.

But the lizards had heard Max's idea, too, and the very thought of more stings seemed to put a mighty fear into them. "Retreat!" they shouted to one another. "Retreat! Every lizard for himself!"

One by one, the Dracos flung themselves off the tower and out over the cliff. Even the ones who lay groaning at the tower's base pulled themselves to their feet and joined their comrades. Wing-flaps spread, they glided along the coast until they vanished from view.

Alexis and Buzz landed at the tower top.

"That was incredible," Buzz said breathlessly. "We did it. I can't believe it!"

"No," said Max, looking at the spot where the lizards had disappeared. "I'm not sure I believe it, either."

"What do you mean?"

Max's brow knitted together. "Well, didn't this victory seem kind of easy to you?"

"No battle where good bugs get hurt is ever 'easy,'" Buzz said darkly.

"Sorry. You're right."

But Max found his head was still full of doubts.

The cause had looked lost. There had been dozens of Draco lizards on the tower, and they had already done severe damage. Taking out the bug watchtower would have been a major blow. So why had they turned tail and run so quickly?

"I think Buzz is a little offended," Alexis remarked, once Buzz had left to call the troops to order.

"I know. I didn't mean to offend her. I'm just kind of suspicious."

"Go on."

"It all comes down to one question. Why would those Draco lizards come all the way to Bug Island just to be scared off at the first sign of trouble?"

Before they could talk any more, Buzz

came in for one of her high-speed stunt landings. "We're heading back to Bug Base Camp to get ready for the parade," she announced brightly. "Want an IAF escort?"

"Gladly!"

Buzz's cheerful tone told Max his comment was already forgotten. But the doubts still lingered in his mind. There were still many more Draco lizards out there, lurking in the treetops.

Bug Base Camp was bustling with activity. All the bugs were full of excitement and pride, and the news of the IAF victory at the watchtower just added to it. Max watched them hanging up banners made from webbing, going through parade ground drills, polishing one another's plating, and marching in formation.

Webster popped up in front of him without warning, as he so often did. "Hi, M-Max! Want to help me put some decorations up?"

Max sighed. "Not right now, Webster. I'm not really in the mood."

"But it's a celebration. Everyone's helping out," said Spike, who had waddled over to join them.

"What's the m-matter?" Webster asked.

"I just can't shake the feeling that something's wrong."

Webster patted Max on the shoulder. "I get that feeling a lot," the spider admitted.

"Everyone says it's my n-nerves. Maybe you've got n-nerves, too."

"I guess."

"It's going to be fine!" Spike boomed. "Now, come and give my armor a polish and stop being such a worrywart."

Max put his thoughts aside and pitched in with the preparations, but whenever he could, he climbed up to the battlements and looked out over the forest. As night fell, Max peered into the distance and Alexis floated up by his side.

"Still thinking about the Dracos?"

"I can't stop," Max said. "In fact, I think we should go on a quick scouting mission."

"If that's what you need to cheer yourself up, sure."

Max and Alexis slipped away, leaving the noise and excitement of the bug camp behind them. They headed out to the tree line, where web lines had been laid to trip up any reptile invaders that came over land. Then they flew past the first of the huge trees, which looked ghostly in the moonlight.

"See anything?" Alexis asked.

"Not so far," said Max. "Let's head on a bit farther."

Up ahead was a crooked, ancient-looking tree draped in vines. It was full of gaping holes where branches had broken off long ago.

"Just a little farther," he said to Alexis. "I think we're getting close to—"

"Close to this!" hissed a voice from above and behind.

In the next second, sharp claws gripped Max. He went tumbling off Alexis's back and down into the leaves. The Draco lizard had swept down as silently as a ninja.

Max fought, but there were more lizards swarming out of the old tree. They pinned him down. Nearby, Alexis had met the same fate.

All he could do was struggle as one lizard came swaggering up to him. It was the one they had fought with before—the one who they had cornered, and who had escaped.

"How nice to see you again." He grinned. "I am Captain Drax. And you have flown right into my trap!"

ALL TIED UP

Drax and his Draco lizards used the decaying tree as their base. Lizard sentries crouched down at the tips of the branches, hiding among the leaves, keeping a lookout.

Max watched, helpless, as two burly lizards bit lengths of vine free and used them to tie his hands and feet. Then they went to work on Alexis.

"Leave him alone!" Max yelled.

"Make us." The lizards grinned. They wrapped vines around Alexis's wings. Max could only watch as the butterfly struggled in vain.

"Earlier on, you wanted me to talk," Captain Drax gloated. "I wasn't in the mood then. But now, I'm feeling pretty chatty. But we'll have to make it quick. Our allies, the birds, will be coming to fetch you and your butterfly companion soon."

Max felt terror grip him as tightly as the vines that held him prisoner.

"Take him to the topmost branches!" Drax ordered. "When the birds come, they'll find him all ready for them."

The lizards dragged Max up and up, all

the way to the very highest branch of a tree. They dragged Alexis over to a second tree and began to hoist him up that one.

"We're keeping you prisoners separate," grunted a lizard, "so you don't get any funny ideas about escaping."

Captain Drax tied Max to a slim branch that hung a long way above the forest floor. "Break the branch or slip your bonds, and you'll fall all the way down," the lizard said.

They left him alone, laughing all the while. Max craned his neck around, trying to see where Alexis had gone. He spotted a brief shimmer of blue among the branches of the neighboring tree—too far away to reach, even if he'd been untied.

Max wracked his brain to think of some clever way out of this jam. Nothing came to mind. As Max lay there, stuck to the flimsy branch, he overheard the whining voices of lizards down below.

The Draco lizards were swaggering around, overjoyed with their success. "Can you believe it?" hissed one of them. "Who cares that we didn't take down the watchtower when we've captured Max himself!"

"We never meant to take down the watchtower," snarled a bigger lizard.

Max pricked up his ears

"So, why'd we attack it, then?" the smaller lizard asked.

"To make the bugs think the watchtower was the target, that's why. If they knew what our real target was, they'd come after us in a wingbeat."

Max lay very still in the moonlight and tried to breathe as quietly as he could. *Keep talking*, he thought. *Don't mind me.*

Suddenly, a different voice interrupted. "What are you scaly beasts gossiping about?" Captain Drax snapped.

"This soldier doesn't understand his orders," sneered the big Draco lizard.

Captain Drax took a deep breath through his nostrils. It sounded like he was about to breathe fire on his troops.

"Very well, let's go over it *again*." He seethed. "Tomorrow, during the bug parade, our bird allies will snatch General Barton and take him to Reptile Island. Our job is to keep the insects busy and draw their attention away, so the birds can make a surprise attack. Have you all got that?"

"Yes, sir," came the response from the gathered lizards.

"Good!"

Suddenly, Max realized the extent of the lizards' plan. "I've got to get out of here," he whispered to himself. "Barton is in danger!"

He looked down at the dizzying drop below him. The tree he was in was old and probably dead, so the weaker branches should break. He could bounce the branch up and down until it snapped, but then how would he survive the fall?

Suddenly, something tickled the back of his neck.

He jerked away in panic. "Get off me!"

Max expected to see a lizard trying to take a sneaky bite out of him. But it wasn't a lizard. Max was staring at a small, dark beetle, peeking out from a hole in the branch.

"Keep your voice down," it whispered. "I'm here to help."

Excitement gripped Max. "You're a deathwatch beetle!"

"Yes!" The beetle bowed. "Let me introduce myself. I am Grim. I'm going to get you out of here!"

Max remembered that deathwatch beetles were a kind of wood-boring beetle. In their larval stage, they ate their way through decaying wood. As adults, they were known to make a ticking noise by banging their heads against wooden surfaces.

"Hold still," the beetle whispered. "I'll get rid of those vines."

Max didn't move a muscle as Grim clambered over his body. He listened intently. From somewhere nearby came the hissing sound of lizard voices. Then there was the low, steady munching of Grim chewing through his bonds, and the tickle of his legs as he scurried over him. After only a few minutes, the tight grip on his wrists loosened. Max tugged one hand free and held on tightly to the branch. Grim kept munching, and with a sudden snap, the last of the vines went tumbling silently down to the forest floor.

"Now follow me," Grim said. "Don't make a sound."

Max inched back along the branch toward the tree trunk. His knee broke a twig off with a crack. The sound of lizard voices suddenly stopped.

Max pressed himself flat down on the tree branch so he wouldn't be seen.

"What was that?" muttered one of the lizards.

"It's probably just one of the deathwatch beetles ticking away inside this old tree," said another. "Rotten old thing is infested with them."

Phew, thought Max.

At the end of the branch was a tiny hole

leading into the tree. Grim led the way and Max wiggled through behind him. It smelled of musty, damp wood. Max prayed he wouldn't sneeze.

"Welcome to my home," Grim said.

"I can't see a thing in here!" Max whispered.

"Not to worry. Just put your hand on my shell and follow me down. If we get separated, I'll make a ticking noise so you can find me again."

Max set off on a strange, blind journey through complete darkness. He shuffled along behind Grim, down through the winding tunnels that the deathwatch beetles had eaten away through the dead wood.

It wasn't long before the ticking began. Max knew that deathwatch beetles made their tick-tock noise to attract mates, but he hadn't expected to hear it from all around, deafeningly loud. To keep his mind focused in the dark and the confusion, he thought of Barton, who still had no idea of the attack that was coming. And he kept his hand firmly on Grim's bobbing back.

Most of the time, his feet pressed against soft, rotting wood, but more than once he stepped on something squishy.

"Eep!" yelped something below him.

"Please be careful of the larvae," Grim said.

"Sorry!" Max said.

"That's my family you're stepping on," groused another beetle.

I wish Glower was here to light the way, Max thought. *Or Roxy. Grim doesn't seem to understand humans can't see in near darkness!*

To his relief, Max finally caught sight of the moonlit forest again, through a gaping hole between the tree roots.

"Freedom," he whispered. "Thanks, Grim. I owe you big time."

"I'm just doing my part," Grim said modestly.

Max turned to leave—and then a thought struck him. He might be free, but Alexis wasn't.

He needed to warn Barton. With every

second that passed, dawn was drawing closer. With the dawn, the birds would come.

But if he ran to find Barton now, he'd be abandoning Alexis to his fate . . . He had to do something, now.

HIGH-SPEED ESCAPE

Max thought about how Alexis had saved his life by catching him in mid-air, and made up his mind.

"We can't leave yet, Grim. Alexis is trapped in that tree up there. We have to rescue him."

"Of course! Never leave a bug behind. That's the Battle Bug motto." Grim paused.

"I think we'll need a few more of us, in case there's trouble. I'll go get the rest of my family."

Grim vanished inside the dead tree. Within minutes, he came back out again, followed by two more deathwatch beetles. Then three more after that. Then six, then eight. Max looked on, astonished, as a scuttling flood of little beetles emptied out of the tree. *There must be* hundreds *of them,* he thought.

"Deathwatch clan ready!" Grim said with a smart salute.

"Grim, when you said you'd get your family, I didn't think you meant your *whole* family!"

The beetles poured up the tree where

Alexis was being held prisoner. Two of them carried Max between them. It was like he was surfing on a giant wave of beetles.

Luckily, it was easy to spot the butterfly, even at night. His wide blue wings could be seen from far away. One of them fluttered weakly, as if it had been injured.

Max warned Grim to look out for lizard guards, but they didn't seem to have posted any.

"It looks like the lizards thought you were the more valuable prisoner," Grim said.

The moment they reached Alexis, Max went to untie him. "How badly are you hurt?" he asked anxiously.

"Not at all," Alexis said, fluttering his wings. "I just pretended I was to fool those lizards."

"So we can fly out of here?"

"Yes. Max, these reptiles are a menace. I've changed my mind. I'm not going back to my glade after all. I'm going to take you back to camp and stay to fight."

"That's great!" Max cheered.

Just then, a roar of rage went up from the old decayed tree where the lizards were based.

"Looks like they've noticed you're missing," said Alexis.

The lizards launched themselves from the neighboring tree, one by one. They whizzed through the air like deadly little darts, scrambling over the branches with frightening speed.

"You'd better get going, fast," Grim said. "No time for good-byes. Warn Barton."

Max threw his leg over Alexis's back. "Thanks for everything, Grim. I owe you one."

As Alexis flew, his powerful wings beat so fast that Max had to hang on for dear life.

"There they are!" a lizard behind them called. Max grimaced. Once again, Alexis's striking colors had made him easy to spot, but this time it had worked against them.

Now that the lizards knew where to go, the entire troop of them came after Max and Alexis in a hissing storm. From branch to branch they zipped, clung, and flew again.

Alexis was only just keeping ahead of them. Max glanced back and saw the lizards were closing in fast. Any moment now, they'd catch up, and Max's only chance to warn Barton would be lost.

"Can you fly any faster?" he yelled.

"I'm going as fast as I can!" Alexis gasped. "We butterflies are built for agility, not speed."

Max thought of all the butterflies he'd ever seen fluttering gracefully around the flowers in Grandpa Mike's garden. Maybe that agility could help them now.

"I've got an idea. Head over to the web barricades."

"Are you serious? We barely made it through last time."

"Trust me," Max urged.

Alexis changed course. The lizards veered around to follow and were back in hot pursuit. Soon, the cloudy gray shapes of spider webs appeared, marking the edge of the trapped area.

"Here we go," Alexis said grimly. "Hold on tight."

The brave butterfly zipped through the first hole in the web, darted up, and powered through a second gap.

"Can't stop!" howled a lizard from behind them. Max looked back to see it struggling to turn and reach the hole in time. It missed. The lizard crashed headlong into many sheets of sticky web. He hung there, help-less, looking like a sticky rubber toy that'd been thrown against a window.

The other lizards were more careful. Three of them made it through the first hole and grabbed onto a branch, preparing to leap and glide again.

Alexis bobbed and swerved, threading through the smallest gaps he could find. The lizards tried to follow, but one of them couldn't even pull his legs off the sticky branch, while the other two messed up their glides and tumbled down into the soft, gluey webs.

Like lizards landing in cotton candy, Max thought.

One by one, the Draco lizards got caught in the webs. They were fierce, but not a single one of them could match Alexis's flying skill. By the time Max and Alexis flew out of the last of the web traps, only one Draco lizard was still following: Captain Drax.

"Looks like you're all out of barricades, human," Drax snarled. He swooped toward them.

Max leaned away at the last possible second, and Drax sailed past overhead. The lizard banked around in flight and came back for another pass.

Max looked down, wondering where they were. He saw familiar-looking blooms in scarlet, blue, and gold, along with several pairs of toothy green jaws. "The Forbidden Glade!" he cried.

"Just when I thought things couldn't get any worse," Alexis wheezed. The butterfly was running out of steam.

Max could think of only one thing to try. If it failed, both he and Alexis were doomed.

"I've got an idea, but it's dangerous," he said.

"Do it!"

Drax swept past again, drawing closer this time.

Max guided Alexis low to the ground, toward the gaping jaws of a Venus flytrap plant. They flew closer until they were almost within reach of its green mouth.

Max glanced behind them. Drax was incoming.

"Ha!" Drax gloated. "My lizard-born strength is greater than yours, human. Prepare to be eaten!"

Drax hurtled toward them on a collision course. His mouth gaped wide. But the Venus flytrap was gaping even wider.

Alexis flew between the open jaws. His legs almost brushed the trigger hairs. Then Max signaled Alexis to change direction suddenly, swooping up just before Drax caught them.

Drax realized, too late, that he'd been tricked. He tried to fly up, but the angle was too steep and he belly flopped into the Venus flytrap's open mouth.

He wiggled and twisted around, desperate to escape, and crashed into the trigger hairs.

The jaws began to close.

"Noooo!" Drax howled, but it did no good. The jaws clamped shut, trapping him inside.

PARADE PANIC

Faintly, in the far distance, Max heard the thunder of hundreds of birds' wings rising to fill the sky.

"I think our problems may only just be beginning," said Alexis. "Look. The sun's rising."

"We need to warn Barton. Let's go!" Max cried.

Soon, they reached the bug parade ground, an open square that seemed to be bigger than a football field. It was surrounded with burrows and little mounds. Bugs of all kinds were gathered in groups, forming into squares and lines, practicing for the parade.

The air above the ground was crowded, too. Wasps, hornets, and bees zipped past one another, showing off their flying skills. Flies circled in huge swarms. Max could hardly see a thing through it.

"I don't see Barton anywhere," Alexis said.

"Bring us down near the scorpions, then, so I can find Spike," Max told Alexis.

When the pair of them landed at the edge of the bug parade ground, the bugs looked at them in amazement.

"What happened to you guys?" asked an ant. "Barton's been looking for you, Max."

Spike was parading with his friends in the scorpion division. As soon as he saw Max land, he broke formation and barged through the bug ranks to reach him.

"Little buddy! Where have you been?"

"It's a long story," Max said. "No time to explain. Where's Barton?"

Spike jabbed his stinger at a mound of earth in the middle of the square. A swarm of bees bustled in the air above it. "He's supposed to give his speech from up there in five minutes. The Elite Bee Guard is doing a flyby."

Max climbed onto Spike's back and they tried to push through the masses of bugs to reach the hill.

It was slow going. The parade ground was just too crowded. Insects and arachnids from all across Bug Island covered every bit of ground. With the IAF practicing above, there was no way to fly straight there, either.

"Sorry about this," Spike said to the bugs in front of him. "COMING THROOOOOUGH!"

With that, he charged. He went through the smaller bugs like a snowplow, sending them flying to the left and right. Bugs yelled, buzzed, and squealed in annoyance, but Spike ignored them.

General Barton crawled up to the top of the hill and looked down on the gathered bug crowds. "My fellow bugs, large and

small, we are assembled here today for one important purpose . . ."

Max looked to the horizon. Distant winged shapes were coming into view.

"General!" he yelled at the top of his voice, hoping he was close enough for Barton to hear.

Barton stopped. "Max? Is that you? Excellent. I was worried you wouldn't make it."

"General, get to cover. It's an air raid. The birds are attacking!"

"What?" Barton looked up, just in time to see the first of the birds come swooping over the treetops.

Behind him, two enormous stag beetle bodyguards leaped into action. One of them

stood bravely in front of Barton, protecting
him with his whole body, while the other
flew up into the air to meet the bird attack.
The Elite Bee Guard buzzed with one voice,
swarming in a cloud above their general.

"Battle Bugs!" bellowed Barton. "Battle
stations!"

AIR ATTACK

The hornets, already in the air for their stunt-flying exercises, shot up to engage the birds. Several divisions of wasps followed them.

The hornet squadron crashed through the birds' attack path. The birds had size on their side, but the hornets had numbers. They jabbed their stingers at the birds from all sides, and the birds couldn't defend themselves. Soon, injured birds were retreating . . .

A small group of birds made it through the hornet barrage.

"Those birds are bee-eaters," Max told Alexis. "We have to send the Elite Bee Guard back to the ground."

Max scrambled down from Spike's back and onto Alexis's. Boy and butterfly soared up into the chaos of the air fight.

With birds and insects screaming past overhead in all directions, it was hard to tell what was going on. Max saw Buzz flying circles around a furious bee-eater and a bird snatch a wasp out of the sky.

"I have to find Barton," he said to himself.

He and Alexis flew across to where the bees had been flying moments before.

The group of birds who had made it this far was making short work of Barton's Elite Bee Guard, just as Max had feared. They swept in, attacked, and zoomed back up into the sky before turning around for another run.

"Land!" Max shouted to the remaining bees. "You've got to get out of the air."

"We'll be helpless on the ground," a bee warrior shouted angrily.

"No you won't. They only catch prey that's flying. If you land, they'll leave you alone."

The Elite Bee Guard ducked out of the fight, settling down on the ground among the other bugs.

Max finally saw Barton himself, standing bravely between his two stag beetle bodyguards. Three bee-eaters were heading straight for him.

"The general's open to attack," he told Alexis. "Those bees were meant to be his air cover, and now they're gone."

"Let's rush the birds!" Alexis said. "I'm a Battle Bug. My general needs me."

The butterfly's bravery gave Max a lump in his throat.

"It wouldn't help," he said quietly. "We can't reach Barton in time. We're too far away."

I'm going to lose for the first time ever, he thought.

As if to prove him right, a familiar tugging feeling began in his pocket. He knew what it was. The magnifying glass was try-ing to pull him away from Bug Island, as it always did when his work here was done.

"That can't be it!" he yelled. "I'm not fin-ished here . . . There has to be more I can do!"

He angrily pulled the magnifying glass out. It was glowing like the pages of the book did. As the sunlight struck the lens, a beam of concentrated light sprang from the other side. It was so bright he could barely look at it.

Max tilted the beam around, full of a sense of wonder. How could this be happen-ing? No ordinary magnifying glass could focus the sun's rays into a beam that bright. It just wasn't possible.

But then, this was no ordinary magnifying glass.

"It's not calling me back home at all," he whispered. "It's showing me the answer."

The three bee-eater birds were seconds away from reaching Barton. Max carefully angled the dazzling beam of light until it shone right into the eyes of the oncoming birds.

Suddenly, they screeched in terror. "I'm blinded!" yelled one, flying away on a crazy zigzag course.

"What is that light?" another howled before flapping away in fear.

The third bird screeched and dive-bombed, disappearing into nearby trees.

"That was amazing!" Alexis said in awe.

"Watch this!" Max shone the beam up into the sky, where the birds and hornets were still fighting a desperate battle.

The flickering, blinding light sent the remaining birds into a total panic. They abandoned the fight and fled. Their terrified screeches echoed all around the forest, and were still ringing in the distance long after the last of them was gone.

As Max laughed and watched them fly away, he suddenly remembered seeing a TV commercial for shiny reflective tape streamers—bird scarers.

Birds are frightened of flashing lights, he thought. *I should have remembered sooner!*

It was a very relieved Barton who climbed to the top of the hill and delivered his speech. This time, he got to finish it.

Max stood by his side as the parade went by after he was done speaking. As the pair of them watched wave after wave of proud fighting bugs troop past, antennae and stingers held high, Max felt more confident than ever.

"We *will* win this war, no matter what the reptiles throw at us," Barton said.

"I was just thinking the same thing," Max said. "Oops. My magnifying glass is pulling again. This time it really means it."

Barton laughed. "Get some rest. We'll take it from here."

The strange forces of the *Encyclopedia* pulled Max back up into the sky and into his own world again. Max couldn't wait to try out the idea he'd had on Bug Island.

He pushed open the shed door. There was Grandpa Mike, standing by the blueberry patch with an amused look on his face.

"Now, what were you up to in there?"

"Oh, bug stuff," Max said lightly. "Grandpa, I think I've figured out how to solve the bird problem."

Grandpa Mike raised an eyebrow. "Oh?"

Later that afternoon, Max stood with his hands on his hips, proudly watching his brand-new reflective streamers shimmering in the sun. The greedy birds watched him from far off in the sky, too scared of the flickering lights to come any closer.

"What do you think?" he asked.

"Very clever," Grandpa Mike said. "Now that the berries are safe, let's go watch that bug documentary you were telling me so much about."

Max grinned. TV bugs weren't quite as cool as watching the Battle Bugs in action, but they'd have to do for now!

REAL LIFE BATTLE BUGS!

Queen Alexandra's birdwing butterfly

The Queen Alexandra's birdwing is an impressive and brightly colored butterfly. It is the largest in the world, with a wingspan of up to eleven inches. It lives exclusively in northeastern Papua New Guinea. This rare, endangered species is found in a thin strip of low-lying coastal rain forest, and nowhere else.

Although it had previously been known to local inhabitants, the butterfly was given its current name by Europeans in the early twentieth century. It was named *Alexandra* after Alexandra of Denmark.

The birdwing exhibits strong sexual dimorphism, which means that the male and female of the species look very different. The female is by far the larger, but the male is much more colorful. The female is mostly a dark brown color, with a yellow body, and small, yellow-white triangles on her wings. The male has striking blue-green wings, with dark black stripes and a bright yellow abdomen.

Deathwatch beetle

The deathwatch is a type of wood-boring beetle that is native to northern Europe, but is also sometimes found in North America. Because young larvae of the species bore into dead, dry wood, they can be unwittingly transported from one place to another, and become serious pests.

These beetles are known for the noises they make. Once inside a piece of timber, they bash their heads against the wood to create their signature tapping sound. If you live in a house with this so-called "woodworm," you may have experienced this annoying sound while trying to fall asleep—deathwatch beetles tend to be most active during the night.

Sound is a great way to communicate if you live in complete darkness like the death-watch. However, the regular tapping gave rise to superstitions about the insects. Some people used to believe that the beetles were a bad omen, and that the sound they emitted was a countdown to death! But now we know the tapping noise the beetles make is just to attract potential mates.

MAX'S ADVENTURE CONTINUES!

Turn the page for a special sneak peek!

MAX'S ADVENTURE CONTINUES!

SHORTCUT

Max landed with a thud. His sneakers crunched on gritty, sloping rock and skidded out from under him. With a yell, he fell on his backside and slid even farther down the slope. With one flailing hand he caught hold of a rock and hung on to it until he'd stopped sliding.

"Ouch," he yelled as he came to a bumpy halt.

He struggled to his feet and dusted himself off. It was always a bit of a bumpy landing on Bug Island, but this time was even harder. The rocky slopes of Fang Mountain were not exactly a feather bed.

Max looked out at the amazing view over Bug Island. In the dim light of the morning, everything was calm and quiet. He listened for the telltale sound of crickets and other bugs, but he couldn't hear a thing.

The silence gave him a creepy feeling, as if he'd arrived too late for some important battle.

"Weird," Max whispered to himself. Part

of him was relieved. At least he wasn't in the middle of a vicious reptile assault. The recent bird raid was still fresh in his memory. Bee-eaters loaded with flying Draco lizard troops had almost overwhelmed the Battle Bugs, and only Max's quick actions had saved the day.

"Better make my way to Bug Camp," Max said to himself. "They'll know what's going on." He looked down and saw the forest stretching out below him. Farther off to the south, he could make out the curve of the bay, and then the forest, where the bugs usually lived.

The only way to reach the forest was to descend the slopes of Fang Mountain, and Max didn't have a bug's advantages when it came to climbing. He picked his way down the gentler slopes easily enough, but the steeper drops were more treacherous. He hunkered down on his hands and knees, spreading his weight out as evenly as he could so he wouldn't fall.

Max was soon sweating from the effort of the climb, and the forest didn't seem to be getting any nearer. What he needed was a lift from a flying friend, like Buzz the hornet air ace, or even Alexis the giant butterfly.

He came to a halt on a rocky ledge and peered over the side. Then, he saw something that would help him: hanging vines dangling downward, looking as thick as rope.

"That's more like it." Max grinned. "Time to take a shortcut!"

Max took hold of a length of vine and braced his feet against the rock face. He remembered abseiling the indoor climbing wall with his Scout troop, and gently lowered himself down the rock wall, taking care to keep a good grip on the vine.

He glanced down as he climbed. The ground looked very far away, and the breeze made him swing in the air. Below, he spotted a narrow rock ledge with a little tree sprouting from the cliff just above. From there he might be able to make his way down to the forest.

However, as he pushed off the rock face with his legs, the vine made an ominous creaking noise. Then came a cracking, splitting sound.

"Uh-oh," Max cried. "I'm only half-way down!"

He frantically tried to climb down faster, but it was too late. The vine broke free from the side of the rock with a dry rattle of falling earth.

"Argh!" Max cried as he fell. In an instant he tumbled through the air and crashed through the branches of the little tree below. Before he could get his bearings, the branches split, and he went crashing to the rock ledge. The vine rope landed on top of him in a loose heap.

"Owww," he yelled for the second time this morning. "What's with today?"

He pulled himself upright again, wincing. The narrow ledge had even less room to move than he'd had before, and although he'd thought it might be easier to reach the forest from here, the sheer drop below made his heart lurch. He was stuck, he realized, with no way down and no way back up.

"Looks like you're trapped, strange bug," hissed a sinister voice from behind him.

Max spun around, his heart thumping in his chest.

"What the—" he began. But as he looked, all he could see was the tree he'd crashed through and the rocky mountain face. He narrowed his eyes and peered closer. He could've sworn the voice had come from near the tree.

"Over here," he heard the voice tease. "Or am I over here . . . ?"